# I Am
# Just Right

# I Am
# Just Right

David McPhail

I Like to Read®

HOLIDAY HOUSE • NEW YORK

I LIKE TO READ is a registered trademark of Holiday House Publishing, Inc.

Copyright © 2019 by David McPhail
All Rights Reserved
HOLIDAY HOUSE is registered in the U.S. Patent and Trademark Office.
Printed and bound in December 2019 at Tien Wah Press, Johor Bahru, Johor, Malaysia.
The artwork was created with watercolor over pen and ink.
www.holidayhouse.com
First Edition
3 5 7 9 10 8 6 4

This book has been officially leveled by using the F&P Text Level Gradient™ Leveling System.

Library of Congress Cataloging-in-Publication Data
Names: McPhail, David, 1940– author, illustrator.
Title: I am just right / David McPhail.
Description: First edition. | New York : Holiday House, [2019] Summary: A boy who is too big for his crib, his tricycle, and being picked up by his grandfather is just the right size for his bed, bicycle, and Grandpa's hugs.
Identifiers: LCCN 2018001166 | ISBN 9780823441068 (hardcover)
Subjects: | CYAC: Size—Fiction. | Growth—Fiction.
Classification: LCC PZ7.M478818 Iaam 2019 | DDC [E]—dc23 LC record available at https://lccn.loc.gov/2018001166

ISBN: 978-0-8234-4575-2 (paperback)

*For Little Ben and his grandfather Big Ben*

I am too big for my crib.

I am too big for my shirt.

I am too big for my shoes.

I am too big for my tricycle.

I am too big for
Grandpa to pick up.

But I am just right
for him to hug.

I am just right for my bed.

I am just right
for my new shirt.

And I am just right
for my new shoes.

I am just right for my bike.

I am just right for my sister.

I am just right for this book.

I am just right.

# I Like to Read®

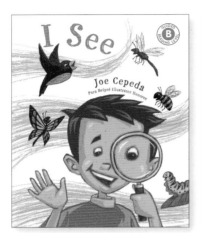

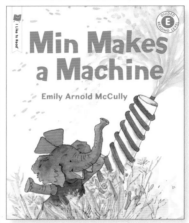

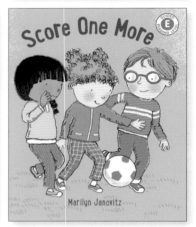

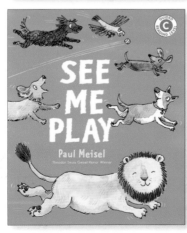

**5**

**Visit HolidayHouse.com/ILiketoRead** for more about I Like to Read®
books, including flash cards, reproducibles, and the complete list of titles.